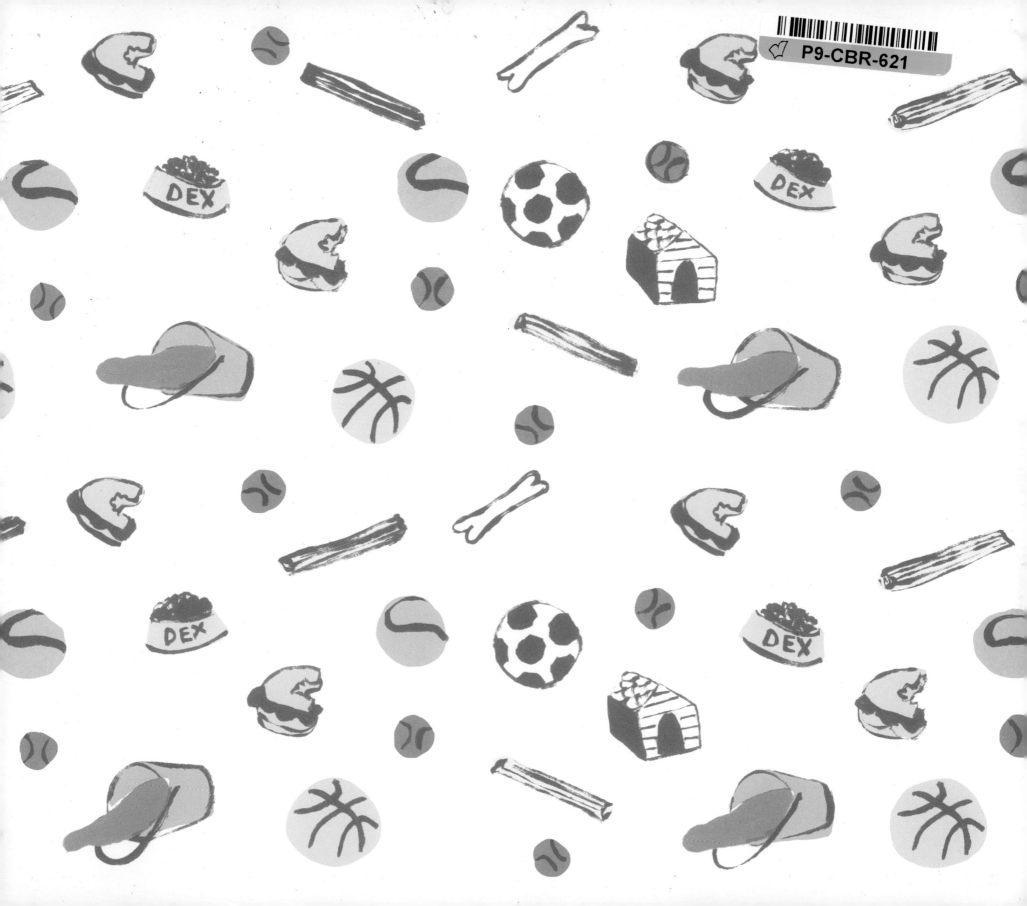

For Ben
- CKS

For Oliver
- KB

TELL TAIL

Written by C.K. Smouha

Illustrated by Katie Brosnan

Dex wasn't like the other dogs in his family.

His dad was strong and tough
with a big, loud bark. His brothers,
Rex and Lex, liked to run and
jump and fight and his mum was
a champion digger.

But Dex liked playing and painting and chatting. And when he did any of those things, his tail would wag...

A LOT...

... which his family found very embarrassing.

No matter how hard he tried,
Dex couldn't get his tail to behave.

When he spotted a ball,
his tail wagged like crazy.

When he sniffed his dinner,
his tail wagged like crazy.

When Dad came home,
his tail wagged like crazy.

Until Dad told him off.

Then Dex's tail tucked itself between his legs and wouldn't come out.

Dex's family tried to help.
'Use your words,' said Mum.

STOP WAGGING ALL OVER THE PLACE YOU STUPID THING!

But his tail wouldn't listen.

'Exercise your mind,' said Dad.

But his tail took no heed.

'Give it a nip,' said his brothers.

But Dex's tail thought he was playing
a game and wagged even more.

Sunday was the family outing to the park. Dex sat firmly on his tail and stared straight ahead.

This time I won't let my tail embarrass me.

Dad found a squirrel and started barking really loudly.

Mum dug a hole and disappeared
inside it, Rex got into a fight and
Lex won a race.

Dex sat perfectly still.

A cat ran past.

Dex didn't flinch.

Someone
d
r
o
p
p
e
d
a sandwich.

Dex squeezed his eyes shut and
breathed through his mouth.

A big red dog bounded up to him,
but Dex stared straight ahead.

He waited for Bailey to go away.

But Bailey didn't go away.

He bounced up and down
in front of Dex.

He had the biggest... reddest...

fluffiest...

... most ridiculous tail
Dex had ever seen.

It wagged so wildly that Dex
couldn't help himself.

He just had to join in.

Dex was having such a brilliant time
that he forgot all about his tail woes.

But one look from Dad reminded him.

Dex ran away as fast as
he could.

He ran.

And ran.

And ran.

He ran so hard and so fast
that he ran out of breath.
He ran out of energy.

He ran out of
everything.

He couldn't even lift his tail.

It was a relief.

Mum and Dad and Rex and Lex
looked high and low for Dex.

DEEEXXX!

In the far distance, Dex heard Dad
and hauled himself to his feet.

'There you are,' said Mum,
'we were looking everywhere.'
'Sorry,' said Dex.
His tail was completely still.

'Well,' said Dad, 'aren't you
happy to see us?'
'Yes,' said Dex.

But his tail didn't flinch.

At home, everything went
back to normal.

Dad went to work, Rex and Lex
got into the usual trouble and
Mum worked on a particularly
big hole in the garden.

Dex went to school and ate his
dinner and did his homework,
with no further trouble from
his tail.

It didn't wag and it didn't tuck under.
It was perfectly motionless at all times.

After a few weeks, Dad began to feel a little uneasy.

Nobody else seemed to notice, but Dad couldn't shake the feeling that something wasn't right.

'Come on son,' said Dad, 'let's go to the park.'

'This is nice,' said Dad.
'Yes,' said Dex. But his tail didn't budge.

'Is everything okay Dex?' asked Dad.
'Everything's fine Dad,' said Dex.

'Okay,' said Dad, and turned to go.

But just then, they caught sight of a flash of red through the trees...

Bailey was so happy to see Dex,
it looked like his tail might take
off into the air.

DEX!

Dad and Dex stared, dumbfounded, but Bailey didn't care.

He really, really didn't care at all.

And then suddenly, Dex snapped.
With a deep growl, he leapt at Bailey.

They rolled…

skidding

and tumbling…

...straight into the duckpond.

They blinked at each other
in stunned silence, until
a strange sound brought
Dex to his senses.

It was Dad.
He was laughing.

And what's more,
his tail was...

wagging!

Hesitantly at first, Dex's tail began to wag too.

Bailey, Dex and Dad had a marvellous afternoon.
Dex and Bailey taught Dad all their favourite games.

And Dad remembered a few more that he had played when he was just a pup.

The sun was sinking low
as Dad and Dex headed home,
the sky a deep shade of orange.

Tomorrow would be a lovely day.

Tell Tail

Text © C K Smouha
Illustrations © Katie Brosnan

British Library Cataloguing-in-Publication Data.

A CIP record for this book is available from
the British Library.
ISBN: 978-1-908714-86-2
First published in the UK, 2020 and USA, 2021

Printed in Poland

Cicada Books Ltd
48 Burghley Road
London, NW5 1UE
www.cicadabooks.co.uk